W9-BUI-696

LANZAROTE

A poet, essayist and novelist, Michel Houellebecq is the author of three previous novels, *Whatever* (*Extension du domaine de la lutte*), *Atomised* (*Les Particules élémentaires*), winner of the Prix Novembre and the 2002 International IMPAC Dublin Literary Award, and *Platform* (*Plateforme*). He lives in Ireland.

ALSO BY MICHEL HOUELLEBECQ

Whatever
Atomised
Platform

Michel Houellebecq

LANZAROTE

TRANSLATED FROM THE FRENCH BY
Frank Wynne

VINTAGE BOOKS
London

Published by Vintage 2004

17

Copyright © Flammarion 2000
Translated from the French, *Lanzarote*
Translation copyright © Frank Wynne

Michel Houellebecq has asserted his right under the Copyright, Designs and Patents Act, 1988 to be identified as the author of this work

This book is sold subject to the condition that it shall not by way of trade or otherwise, be lent, resold, hired out, or otherwise circulated without the publisher's prior consent in any form of binding or cover other than that in which it is published and without a similar condition including this condition being imposed on the subsequent purchaser

First published in Great Britain in 2003 by
William Heinemann

Vintage
Random House, 20 Vauxhall Bridge Road,
London SW1V 2SA

www.vintage-books.co.uk

Addresses for companies within The Random House Group Limited can be found at: www.randomhouse.co.uk/offices.htm

The Random House Group Limited Reg. No. 954009

A CIP catalogue record for this book
is available from the British Library

ISBN 9780099448365

Penguin Random House is committed to a sustainable future for our business, our readers and our planet. This book is made from Forest Stewardship Council® certified paper.

Printed and bound in Great Britain by Clays Ltd, Elcograf S.p.A.

'The world is medium-sized.'

Mid-way through the afternoon on 14 December 1999, I realised that my New Year was probably going to be a disaster – as usual. I turned right on to the Avenue Felix-Fauré and walked into the first travel agency I found. The assistant was busy with a customer. She was a brunette wearing some sort of ethnic top; she had had her left nostril pierced; her hair had been hennaed. Feigning a casual air, I began picking up brochures from the displays.

'Can I help you?' I heard after a moment.

No, she couldn't help me; no one could help me. All I wanted was to go home, scratch my balls and leaf through the holiday club brochures; but she had initiated a conversation, I didn't see how I could get out of it.

'I'd like to go away in January . . .' I said with a smile which I imagined to be disarming.

'Do you want to head for the sun?' she shot back at a hundred miles an hour.

'My means are limited,' I continued, modestly.

The transaction between tourist and tour operator – at least from the impression I've formed from reading a number of the trade magazines – tends to transcend the framework of everyday commercial relations – unless such a transaction, dealing as it does with travel, that most dreamlike of commodities, can be said to reveal the true nature – mysterious, profoundly human, almost mystical – of all commercial transactions. Imagine yourself for a moment, dear reader, in the role of the *tourist*. What does it entail? You must listen attentively to the proposals made to you by the professional opposite you. She (usually it is *she*) has at her disposal – such is her job – a broad knowledge of the leisure and cultural opportunities on offer at each of the destinations listed in the brochure; she has a general idea of the clientele, the sports facilities, the opportunities for meeting new people; your happiness – at least your prospect of happiness – during those weeks depends to a degree on her. Her role – far from the stereotypical notion of proposing a 'standard' holiday package, and regardless of the brevity of the encounter – is to discover your expectations, your desires, perhaps even your secret hopes.

'We've got Tunisia. A classic destination and very

affordable in January . . .' she began, to *get into gear*. 'We have southern Morocco, too. It's very beautiful off-season.' *Off-season?* Southern Morocco is beautiful all year round. I knew southern Morocco well, probably a lot better than this stupid bitch. It might very well be beautiful, but it isn't really *my thing*, that was what I needed to get through her thick skull.

'I don't like Arab countries,' I interrupted. 'At least . . .' Thinking about it, I remembered a Lebanese woman I'd met at a swingers club: really hot, nice pussy, big tits too. What's more, a colleague at work had told me about a Nouvelles Frontières hotel in Hammamet, where groups of Algerian women go to enjoy themselves with no men about to spy on them; he had fond memories of the place. Arab countries might well be worth the effort after all, if we could just liberate them from their absurd religion.

'It's not Arab countries I don't like, it's *Muslim* countries,' I went on. 'I don't suppose you have any non-Muslim Arab countries, do you?' It would be a tough question on *Questions pour un champion*: A non-Muslim Arab country . . . you have forty seconds. Her mouth gaped slightly.

'How about Senegal?' she went on, breaking the silence. Senegal. Why not? I'd heard that white men still had great prestige in West Africa. All you had to do to take a girl back to your chalet was show up at a disco; not even a whore, either, she'd do it for the pleasure. Obviously, they welcomed gifts, maybe little gold jewellery; but what woman doesn't appreciate gifts? I couldn't work out why I was thinking about such things; in any case, I didn't feel up to fucking.

'I don't feel up to fucking,' I said. The girl looked up, surprised; it was true that I'd skipped a couple of steps in my train of thought. She went back to shuffling through her brochures. 'Prices for Senegal start at six thousand francs, though . . .' she said. I shook my head sadly. She went to consult another file; they're not brutes, these girls, they're sensitive to financial concerns. Outside on the pavement, passers-by trudged through snow turning slowly into slush.

She came back and sat opposite me and in a frank – and markedly different – tone asked me: 'Have you thought about the Canaries?' Faced with my silence, she explained, with a professional smile: 'People rarely think of the Canaries . . . It's an archipelago off the African coast, warmed by the Gulf Stream; the weather is mild all year round. I've seen people bathing there in January . . .' She gave me some time to digest this information before continuing: 'We have a special offer for Bougainville Playa. One week, all-inclusive, 3,290 francs; departures from Paris on the 9th, 16th and 23rd of January. Superior four-star hotel. All rooms with en-suite bathroom, hairdryer, air conditioning, telephone, TV, mini-bar, room safe, balcony with pool view (or sea view for a supplement), 1000m^2 swimming pool, Jacuzzi, sauna, hammam, fitness centre, three tennis courts, two squash courts, miniature golf, table tennis. Traditional dance shows, excursions from the hotel (details available on site). Travel/cancellation insurance – all-inclusive.

'Where is it?' I couldn't help but ask.

'Lanzarote.'

2

New Year's Eve was a disaster; I tried to hook up to the Internet but I screwed up. I had just moved house; I think I should have reinstalled the card modem or something like that. My fruitless tinkering quickly bored me, I fell asleep at about eleven. A postmodern New Year's Eve.

I had opted for the 9 January departure. At the Relais H in Orly – recently renamed the *Relay* – I bought a number of magazines. *Passion Glisse* offered its usual selection of content. *Paris-Match* dedicated several pages to an article about Bernard-Henri Lévy's book on Jean-Paul Sartre. *Le Nouvel Observateur* had features on teenage sexuality and Prévert's centenary. As for *Libération*, it revisited the Shoah, the duty of memory, the painful exhumation of Sweden's Nazi past. It had hardly been worth changing centuries, I thought. In fact, we hadn't changed centuries; not, at least, according to a linguist in an issue of *Ça se discute* that I'd read the night before; the new century (and incidentally millennium) would not begin until 1 January 2001. From a pedantic point of view he was probably right; but he was obviously just saying it to piss off Delarue. Whether or not the usage was correct, the year 2000 started with a 2, as anyone could see.

The flight over France and Spain went well; I slept almost the whole way. When I woke, the plane was over Portugal, exposing an arid topography. Then it veered towards the ocean. I made another attempt to interest myself in the contents of my magazines. The sun was setting over the Atlantic; I thought about a TV programme I'd seen the night before. In the studio, a porn star contemplated the change of millennium with serenity; to her, men would always be men, what more was there to say? A historian, on the other hand, argued that the concept of the century had a certain relevance, albeit in a metaphorical sense; thus, according to him, the nineteenth century had not actually ended until 1914. A left-wing geneticist hit the roof: it was incredible, indecent, that in the year 2000 so many human beings on the planet were dying of starvation. A right-wing academic commented ironically that while he deplored war and famine as much as the next man, it seemed to him futile to try to change the destiny of mankind unless one could alter the intrinsic nature of man himself; he was, therefore, implicitly in agreement with the porn star, with whom he developed a certain rapport during the programme. But, ill-informed of recent progress in the field of molecular biology, he had no idea that such modific-ation (which he hoped for only inasmuch as he was certain that it was impossible) would very shortly be feasible. For his part, the left-wing geneticist was well aware of these developments; but being a fervent supporter of political protest and democracy, he dismissed such ideas in horror. The debate, in short, simply brought together another bunch of idiots. I slept until the plane landed. From the look of things, I thought to myself, we weren't likely to see the end of the twentieth century for some time.

I have to admit the hotel transfer was well organised. This, then, is what would endure of the twentieth century: science and technology. After all, a Toyota minibus is a far cry from a stagecoach.

3

If it is no match for Corfu or Ibiza in the *crazy techno afternoons* holiday sector, neither is Lanzarote in a position to offer *ecotourism* – for obvious reasons.[1] There is, however, a third possibility open to the island: *cultural tourism* – the sort of tourism of which retired teachers and other mid-market OAPs are so fond. On a Spanish island – in the absence of night-clubs – one might expect to find some vestiges of civilisation (baroque convents, medieval fortresses). Unfortunately, on Lanzarote, all of these beautiful buildings were destroyed between 1730 and 1732 by a succession of earthquakes and volcanic eruptions of unparalleled violence. So, *cultural tourism*, nada.

Considering the limited range of its attractions, it's hardly surprising to find that Lanzarote is patronised by a nebulous variety of tourists – Anglo-Saxon OAPs rub

---

[1] See photos

shoulders with ghostly Norwegian tourists (whose sole *raison d'être* seems to be to give credence to the myth that *you can even see people swimming in January*). Is there anything, in fact, of which Norwegians are not capable? Norwegians are translucent; exposed to the sun, they die almost immediately. Having established the tourist industry in Lanzarote in the early fifties, they deserted the island, located to the far south of their desires – as André Breton might have said on a good day. The islanders have fond memories of them, as is apparent from the menus – the Norwegian wording almost faded with the years – posted at the entrances of long-deserted restaurants. For the remainder of this piece, it will not be necessary to mention Norwegians again.

The same cannot be said of the English, nor of the more general mystery of the English holidaymaker. There is no such mystery to the Germans (who will go anywhere there's sun), still less to the Italians (who will go anywhere there's a cute ass); as for the French,[1]

---

[1] However, I should remind the reader that the *Guides du Routard* (now, alas, also available in Spanish) originated in France, which, by dint of their 'cool' (eco-friendly, humanitarian) attitudes; their passions; their calls for 'intelligent' tourism and for an openness to the unfamiliar (understand before judging); their quasi-frenetic search for an 'authenticity' which is already dying out, have succeeded in redefining international standards of stupidity. I would like to reassure the reader that Lanzarote is not mentioned in the *Guides du Routard*.

let's not even go there. Alone among Europeans in the middle- and higher-income brackets, the English are notable by their absence from mainstream holiday destinations. Nevertheless, meticulous and systematic research, supported by considerable data, makes it possible to map their movements during summer pasturing. They gather in small groups and head for unlikely islands absent from Continental holiday brochures – Malta, Madeira or, indeed, Lanzarote. Once there, they duplicate the principal elements of their home environment right there. When asked to explain their choice of destination, they give answers which are evasive and tautological: 'I came because I came here last year.' It is apparent that the Englishman is not motivated by a keen appetite for discovery. Indeed, one may observe that he is not interested in architecture, landscapes, in anything whatsoever. In the early evening, after a short trip to the beach, he is to be found drinking bizarre cocktails. The presence of the English at a resort, therefore, is no guide to the intrinsic interest of the destination, its splendour or its possible tourist potential. The Englishman goes to a particular tourist destination purely because he is certain that he will meet other Englishmen there. In this, he is diametrically opposed to the Frenchman, a vain creature, so enamoured of himself that the mere sight of a compatriot abroad is anathema to him. For this reason, Lanzarote is a destination to be recommended to the French. It might particularly be recommended to the *hermetic French poets*, who will have plenty of time to produce pieces like:

Shadow,
Shadow of shadow,
Traces on a rock.

Or, more in the style of Guillevic:

Pebble,
Little pebble,
You breathe.

Having dispensed with the case of the *hermetic French poet*, I can now concern myself with the *ordinary French tourist*. Admittedly, in Lanzarote deprived of his habitual *Guide du Routard,* the ordinary French tourist runs the risk of quickly developing all the signs of abject boredom. This would not, one might suppose, pose a problem for the Englishman; but the Frenchman, a vain creature, is also impatient and frivolous. Creator of the sadly renowned *Guide du Routard*, he also, in happier times, perfected the famous *Guide Michelin*, whose ingenious system of star ratings for the first time made it possible for the world to be systematically categorised according to its potential pleasures.

And yet the pleasures of Lanzarote are few: in fact, they are twofold. The first, a little to the north of Guatiza, is the 'Cactus Garden'. Various specimens, selected for their repulsive morphology, are arranged along paths of volcanic rock. Fat and prickly, the cactus symbolises perfectly – not to put too fine a point on it – the abjectness of plant life. Be that as it may, the Cactus Garden is not very large and, as far as I was concerned, our visit could have been be over and done with in somewhat less than half an hour; but I had taken a group excursion and we were obliged to wait for a little moustachioed Belgian. I had passed him as he stood, stock-still, staring at a huge purplish cactus in the shape of a prick, artistically planted next to two smaller, outlying cacti intended to represent its balls. I was struck by his rapt attention: this was certainly a curious phenomenon, but it was hardly unique. Other specimens brought to mind a snowflake, a man sleeping, a ewer. Perfectly adapted to their desert environment, cacti lead, if I may put it thus, a completely unfettered morphological existence. They grow alone for the most part and are therefore not compelled to adapt to the pressures of this or that plant formation. Animal predators, scarce in any case, are immediately deterred by their abundant spines. Such an absence of selective pressures makes it possible for them to develop unhindered into a complex variety of farcical shapes likely to amuse tourists. Their mimicry of the male sexual organ, in particular, always has a certain effect on Italian tourists; but in this moustachioed man, who appeared to be Belgian, things had gone too far; in this man I could discern all the signs of an out-and-out *fascination*.

Lanzarote's second tourist attraction is on a larger scale; it is the high point of any holiday there. I refer to Timanfaya National Park, which is situated at the centre of volcanic activity. Do not be deceived by the words 'national park'; over the twelve square kilometres of the reserve, you are more or less certain not to encounter a single living thing apart from a couple of camels laid on for tourists. In the hotel's chartered minibus, I found myself sitting next to the man with the moustache. After several kilometres, we took a road which ran perfectly straight, carved through the rocky chaos. The first photo opportunity was just before the entrance to the park. Before us, a plain of black rocks with razor-sharp edges stretched out for about a kilometre; there was not a plant nor an insect anywhere. Immediately beyond, the horizon was obstructed by the red, in places almost purple, slopes of the volcanoes. The landscape had not been softened or sculpted by erosion; it was of an utter brutality. Silence fell over the group once more. Beside me, motionless in his 'University of California' sweatshirt and white Bermuda shorts, the Belgian seemed troubled by a confused emotion. 'I think . . .' he said, his voice barely audible; then he was silent. I glanced over at him. Suddenly embarrassed, he crouched down, took his camera from a holdall and began to unscrew the zoom to replace it with a standard lens.

I got back on the minibus; when he climbed aboard again I offered him the window seat; he accepted eagerly. Two German women in dungarees had ventured on to the rocky terrain; they moved with difficulty in spite of their hefty hiking boots. The driver honked the horn several times; they came back to the bus waddling slightly like two fat elves.

*

The remainder of the tour continued in the same vein. The road had been carved out carefully, to the nearest centimetre, between the great walls of jagged rock; at intervals of about one kilometre, open areas had been cleared by bulldozers, these were flagged in advance by road signs displaying a box Brownie. We stopped at each of them; the tourists, spread out across the few square metres of tarmac, made use of their cameras. Aware of the ridiculousness, in their own eyes, of their collective presence in such a confined space, each tried to distinguish himself by his choice of framing. Gradually, bonds formed between the members of the group. Though I myself had not brought a camera, I felt a great solidarity with the Belgian. Had he asked me to help him to change a lens or organise his filters, I would have done so. That's where I stood, vis-à-vis the Belgian. From a sexual point of view, however, I was more attracted to the Germans. They were two stout creatures with heavy breasts. Dykes, probably; but, personally, I enjoy watching two women masturbate and lick each other's pussies; since I have no lesbian friends, it's a pleasure I am usually denied.

The climax of the excursion – as much in the topographical as in the emotional sense – was the stop at the Mirador de Timanfaya Watchtower. To fully appreciate the possibilities of the structure, we had been allocated two hours' free time. This began with a brief talk, given by one of the site employees, intended to highlight the volcanic nature of the surroundings. Cutlets were inserted into a fissure in the rock; they came out grilled. There were gasps and applause. I discovered that the Germans were called Pam and Barbara, the Belgian, Rudi.

Afterwards, there were a number of options. You could buy souvenirs, go to the restaurant and enjoy international cuisine. The more *sportif* could opt for a camel ride.

I turned and saw Rudi near the herd of some twenty beasts. Unaware of the danger, his hands clasped behind his back like a curious child, he walked towards these monsters as they craned their long, lithe, serpentine necks crowned with small cruel heads towards him. Of all the animals in Creation, the camel is unquestionably one of the most aggressive and the most hostile. Few higher mammals – with the exception of certain apes – display such a marked viciousness. In Morocco, tourists attempting to stroke the animals' heads have often had several fingers ripped off. 'I say the lady to be careful,' the camel driver will whine hypocritically. 'Camel not

nice . . .'; the fact still remains the fingers have been
devoured.

'You have to be careful with camels!' I say cheerfully. 'Actually, they're dromedaries.'

'The *Dictionnaire Robert* gives *one-humped camel* or
Arabian camel,' he remarked in a thoughtful tone, not
moving an inch.

Just then, the camel driver reappeared and
viciously rapped the head of the nearest animal which
moved back with a snort of rage.

'Camel ride, mister?'

'No, no, I just wanted a look,' replied Rudi
mysteriously.

The two Germans approached in turn, smiling
excitedly. I quite wanted to watch them climb up on
the camels, but the next trip was in fifteen minutes. To
kill time, I bought a volcano keyring at the souvenir
shop. Later, when we arrived back at the hotel as
twilight descended, I composed the following verse in
homage to the hermetic French poets:

Camel,
Presence of camels,
My minibus lost its way.

'It was a beautiful day,' I thought to myself as I investigated the contents of the minibar back in my room. 'A beautiful day, really . . .' Already it was Monday night. A week on this island would probably be bearable after all. Hardly fascinating, but bearable.

4

'I speak calmly; I live calmly, I sell telephones in
March, in April and September.'
– Gruneberg and Jacobs,
Spanish Through Word Association

On beach holidays, as perhaps in life more generally,
the only truly enjoyable time of day is breakfast. I
helped myself to the buffet three times: chorizo,
scrambled eggs . . . why stint yourself? In any case,
sooner or later I would have to go to the pool. Some
Germans had already spread out their beach towels to
reserve the plastic sunloungers. At the next table, an
enormous hooligan with a skinhead and a moustache
was stuffing himself with cold meats. He was wearing
black leather trousers and a Motorhead T-shirt. The
woman who was with him was frankly indecent, with
her big silicone-enhanced breasts spilling generously
from her miniscule bikini top; triangles of pink latex

that just about covered her nipples. Clouds flitted across the sky. The Lanzarote sky, I was to realise a little later, is continually traversed by clouds which drift to the East with never a shower; it is an island on which it doesn't rain, so to speak, at all. The ideas which have left their mark on the West, whether from Judaea or from Greece, were born under an intangible sky of monotonous blue. It was different here; the sky constantly renewed itself in its very presence.

The lobby of the Bougainville Playa was deserted at this early hour. I went out into the garden and wandered for a few minutes among the plants – which might very well have been bougainvilleas for all I cared. There was a parrot in a cage, staring out at the world with his round and angry eye. The beast was an impressive size – but I'd heard it said that parrots never stop growing and can live to be seventy or eighty years old; some specimens could reach a metre tall. Fortunately, a recent bacterial infection had just dealt with that problem. I passed the cage and had just turned on to a path bordered with flowering shrubs when right behind me I heard someone shout: 'Poor bastard!' I turned round: it was the parrot who was now cackling: 'Poo'Bast'd! Poo'Bast'd!' with growing excitement. I detest birds and for the most part the feeling is mutual; well, if you could call the thing a bird. Even so, it was stupid of him to be such a smart-arse; I'd wrung many a neck for less.

The path continued to wind its way between the flowering shrubs and ended in a small flight of steps at the beach. A Scandinavian man, balancing on the pebbled shore, was slowly performing t'ai chi movements. The water was grey, maybe green, but definitely not blue. The island may well be Spanish, but there was nothing Mediterranean about it, I would simply have to get used to that fact. I walked for a few hundred metres at the water's edge. The ocean was chilly, quite choppy.

Afterwards, I sat on a mound of pebbles. They were black and clearly the product of a volcanic eruption. But unlike the rocks at Timanfaya with their fractal edges, these were round. I held one between my fingers; it felt smooth, you couldn't feel any edges. In three centuries, erosion had already done its work. I lay down, contemplating the conflict, so evident in Lanzarote, between two great forces: the volcano's creation and the sea's destruction. It was a pleasing meditation, in which nothing was at stake, to which no conclusion was possible; I continued in this vein for some twenty minutes.

For a long time, I believed that going on holiday would allow me to *learn the language of the country*; though I was over forty, this illusion had not yet faded completely and shortly before my departure I had bought a copy of the *Marabout Method to Easy Spanish*. The principle of the 'Linkword' word association method was to actively visualise certain images. So, the word for shelf (*estante*), was illustrated thus: 'Imagine a *nest* of *ants* sitting on the shelf'; a drawer (*cajón*): 'Imagine a drawer full of *car horns*'; danger (*peligro*): 'Imagine a *pale, gross* man charging at you: danger!' If the Spanish was close to the French word, the phrase would include a *torero*, a 'typical Spanish person'. So, the word *cero* (zero) was illustrated with the phrase 'Imagine that *toreros* are all just zeros'.

The authors' biases might well explain some of the peculiar turns of phrase, but they couldn't explain some of the examples in the translation exercises, such as: 'My dogs are under the bank' or 'Your doctor wants more money, my dentist wants more cheese.' Though absurdity is amusing for a while, after a certain age it begins to pall, and I must have fallen asleep. When I woke, the sun was at its height, the sky was cloudless; it was almost hot. Two 'techno' beach towels were spread out some metres away. I spotted

Pam and Barbara near the shoreline, up to their waists in the water. They were enjoying themselves: playing piggyback and throwing each other into the water, then tenderly embracing, breast to breast; it was delightful. I wondered where on earth Rudi could be.

The two Germans came back to dry themselves. Close up, Pam seemed slimmer, almost gamine with her short black hair; but Barbara's animal placidity was extraordinary. She had beautiful breasts, I wondered if she'd had them done. I decided she probably had, they were a little too pert when she lay down; but the overall result was very natural, she'd clearly happened on an excellent surgeon.

We talked a little about suntan lotions, the difference between the advertised sun protection factor and the actual protection factor: was it really wise to trust Australian standards? Pam was reading a German translation of a book by Marie Desplechin which could have allowed the conversation to take a literary turn; but I didn't really know what to say about Marie Desplechin, and in any case, Rudi's absence was beginning to worry me. Barbara propped herself on her elbows to join the conversation. I couldn't help looking at her breasts; I realised that I had a hard-on. Unfortunately, she didn't speak a word

of French. '*You have nice breast,*' I said in an approx-
imate English. She smiled broadly and said, '*Thank
you.*' She had long blonde hair, blue eyes and actually
looked like a nice girl. I got to my feet, explaining: '*I
must look at Rudi. See you later . . .*'; then we parted
company, with a little wave.

It was a little after 3 pm, people were finishing
lunch. As I passed the noticeboard, I noticed that there
was a new activity. In addition to the classics, the
Cactus Garden visit and Timanfaya National Park,
today the hotel was offering an excursion to
Fuertaventura by hydroplane. Fuertaventura was the
nearest island, it was low-lying and sandy, the landscape uninteresting; but there were immense beaches
where it was possible to bathe safely; that, at least, was
what I had concluded from the brochure I'd found in
my hotel room. This, I suspected, might explain
Rudi's disappearance; I felt reassured, and I went up to
my room to watch CNN. I like watching television
with the sound turned down, it's a bit like looking at
an aquarium, a prelude to a siesta, but your interest is
still piqued. On this occasion, however, I was having
trouble identifying the war in progress. The clowns on
screen mucking around with their sub-machine guns
seemed too dark-skinned to be Chechens. I tried

fiddling with the colour control, but they were still too dark. Maybe they were Tamils; there was something going on with the Tamils. Subtitles at the bottom of the screen reminded me that this was the year 2000; a fact that was truly astonishing. The transition from the military to the industrial age, predicted as early as 1830 by the founder of positivism, was long in coming to an end. Nevertheless, watching the all-pervading world news, the fact that humanity shared a common calendar and a common destiny was increasingly obvious. Even if it was not in itself significant, the new millennium might well act as a *self-fulfilling prophecy*.

An elephant crossed the screen, reinforcing the Tamil hypothesis, though actually they could be Burmese. In spite of everything, it seemed we were swiftly moving towards the concept of a world federation dominated by the United States, with English as its common language. Of course, the prospect of being governed by fucking idiots was somewhat disagreeable; but it wouldn't be the first time after all. From all the evidence they had left of themselves, the Romans had clearly been a nation of idiots; a fact that hadn't stopped them taking over Judaea and Greece. Then came the barbarians, etc. It was oppressive, this feeling of repetition; I switched over to MTV. MTV without sound is quite bearable; actually, it's quite nice, all those trendy girls wiggling around in their skimpy tops. I ended up taking out my cock and jerking off to a rap video before sinking into sleep for a little more than two hours.

5

At 6.30 pm, I went down to the bar to make the most of *happy hour*. Just as I had decided on a Matador Surprise, in walked Rudi. How could I possibly not invite him to join me? So I did.

'Did you have a good day?' I said casually. 'I assumed you went on the excursion to Fuertaventura.'

'That's right.' He shook his head indecisively before answering: 'It was shit, complete shit. It was boring. And now I've been on every excursion the hotel offers.'

'You're staying a week?'

'No, two weeks,' he said in the voice of one condemned. He was certainly in a fine mess. I offered him a cocktail. While he studied the menu, I had plenty of time to study his face. He had a pallid complexion, despite the days he'd spent in the sun, and worry lines across his forehead. Short, black hair, greying a little, and a bushy moustache. He had a sad, slightly lost expression. I would have said he was around forty-five.

We talked about the island and how beautiful it was. Three Matador Surprises later, I decided to move into more personal territory.

'You've got a slight accent . . . I thought maybe you were Belgian.'

'Not exactly.' A surprising, almost childlike smile appeared. 'I was born in Luxembourg. I'm sort of an immigrant myself . . .' He spoke of Luxembourg as of a lost Eden, though it's common knowledge that it's a minuscule, mediocre country with no distinguishing characteristics – it's not even a country, more an assortment of dummy companies scattered over parkland, nothing but PO boxes for companies with a taste for tax evasion.

It turned out that Rudi was a police inspector and lived in Brussels. He talked bitterly about the city throughout the meal. Delinquency was rife; increasingly, gangs of youths attacked passers-by in the middle of shopping centres in broad daylight. It was better not to even think about what happened at night; for some time now women didn't dare go out alone after dark. Islamic fundamentalism had become alarmingly common; like London, Brussels was now a haven for terrorists. In the streets and the squares, there were more and more women wearing veils. To make matters worse, the conflict between the Flemish and the Walloons had intensified; the Vlaams Blok were close to taking power. He talked of the European capital as of a city on the brink of civil war.

From a personal standpoint, his life was hardly much better. He had married a Moroccan girl, but he and his wife had separated five years ago. She had returned to Morocco, taking their two children; he had not seen them since. All in all, Rudi's life seemed to me to be close to being a total human catastrophe.

Why had he come to Lanzarote? Indecision, he needed a holiday, a pushy travel agent: in short, the classic story.

'In any case, the French despise the Belgians,' he said in conclusion; 'and the worst thing is, they're right. Belgium is an absurd country in steep decline; it is a country which should never have existed.'

'We could hire a car . . .' I suggested to lighten the mood.

He seemed surprised by my suggestion; I became more animated. The island had some spectacular sights; something we had realised on our excursion to

Timanfaya. Admittedly, the inhabitants of Lanzarote didn't seem to realise the fact; but in this they were no different from any other natives. In other ways, it was true, they were strange creatures. Small, shy and sad, they maintained an air of dignity and reserve; they did not correspond to the image of flamboyant Mediterranean peoples so beloved of some Nordic and Batavian tourists. Their sadness seemed to date from long ago; I had discovered in a book on Lanzarote by Fernando Arrabal that the prehistoric peoples of the island had never thought to take to the sea; all that lay, beyond the island's coast, they believed, was uncertainty and error. Of course, they had seen fires rising from other islands, but they had never been curious to see whether these fires had been set by human beings, whether those human beings might be similar to them; avoiding all contact seemed to them the wisest course of action. The history of Lanzarote until recent times was, therefore, a history of complete isolation; and of that history, moreover, nothing remained except the fragmentary tales of a handful of Spanish priests who had gathered some stories before giving their blessing to the extermination of the local population. Such ignorance would later give rise to a number of myths about the origins of Atlantis.

I realised that Rudi was not listening to me; he was finishing his wine, either sedated or pensive. It was true that I had wandered a little off the subject. The people of Lanzarote, I went on enthusiastically, are exactly like all other natives when it comes to beauty. Completely insensible to the splendour of his surroundings, the native generally sets about destroying it, to the anguish of the tourist, a sensitive creature in pursuit of happiness. Once the tourist has pointed out this beauty, the native becomes capable of perceiving it, preserving it and systematising its exploitation in the form of *excursions*. In Lanzarote, however, this process was still in its early stages; it was hardly surprising, therefore, that the hotel offered only three excursions. In which case, why not rent a car? Why not discover these lunar (or Martian, depending on your travel agent) landscapes in comfort? No, the holiday was not over; in fact, it had only just begun.

Rudi immediately agreed to the idea, with considerably more enthusiasm than I had anticipated. The following morning, we went to a car hire company and hired a Subaru for three days. Now, where to go? I had bought a map.

6

'There's the Teguise market . . .' Rudi suggested shyly. 'I have to bring something back for my nieces.' I shot him a baleful glance. I could well imagine the sort of place, with its stalls and its arts-and-crafts shit. But what the hell, it was on the way to the Playa de Famara – by far the most beautiful beach on the island, according to the hotel brochures.

The road to Teguise stretched ahead, impeccably straight, through a desert of alternately black, red and ochre rocks. The landscape was relieved only by the volcanoes in the distance; their hulking presence strangely reassuring. The road was deserted, we drove in silence. It was as though we were in some metaphysical western.

At Teguise, I managed to park near the main square and I settled myself on a café terrace, leaving Rudi to wander around the stalls. It was mostly basketry, pottery and *timples* – a sort of tiny four-string guitar peculiar to the island, according to the hotel leaflets again. I was pretty sure that Rudi was going to buy *timples* for his nieces; that's what I would have done in his position. The most interesting thing was the people visiting the market. There wasn't a single redneck sporting a FRAM cap, nor a single backpacker from the Auvergne. There was a good crowd flocking round the stalls, mostly techno sluts and hippie chicks; you'd think you were in Goa or Bali rather than some godforsaken Spanish island in the middle of the Atlantic. In fact, most of the cafés around the market offered email facilities and cheap Internet connections. At the table next to mine, a tall bearded man in a white linen suit was studying the Bhagavad-gita. His rucksack, also white, was emblazoned with the inscriptions: 'IMMEDIATE ENLIGHTENMENT – INFINITE LIBERATION – ETERNAL LIGHT'. I ordered an octopus salad and a beer. A young guy with long hair wearing a white T-shirt adorned with a multicoloured star came up to me with a small sheaf of leaflets. '*No thanks*,' I said quickly in English. To my surprise, he responded in French. 'They're free, monsieur. It's a series of fun questions to help you discover your true personality.' I took a leaflet from him. Eternal Light, buried in his reading, loftily dismissed the offer. There were about ten of them handing out leaflets in the market.

They didn't pussyfoot about. In large letters on the front page were the words 'AZRAELIAN RELIGION'. I'd heard about the sect before: it was run by a certain Philippe Leboeuf, an ex-hippie columnist for some local paper – *La Montagne,* I think, in Clermont-Ferrand. In 1973, he'd encountered extraterrestrials while visiting the crater at Puy de Dôme. The aliens called themselves Anakim; they had created the human race in a laboratory millions of years ago and followed the progress of their creation from afar. Naturally, they had a message for Philippe Leboeuf, who jacked in his job as a hippie columnist, renamed himself Azrael and founded the Azraelian movement while he was at it. One of the missions conferred upon him was to build an embassy which would serve to welcome the Anakim during their next stay on earth. And there my knowledge of the subject ended; I also knew that the sect was considered relatively dangerous, one to be carefully watched.

The leaflet the guy had given me was perfectly anodyne at any rate. Titled 'Calculate Your Sensual Quotient', it was made up of questions like 'Do you masturbate often?' or 'Have you ever participated in group sex?'; it was the sort of thing you might find in an issue of *Elle*.

Eternal Light's partner came back and sat with him; she'd bought some piece of wicker shit. When she noticed my cigarette, she recoiled in horror; I immediately stubbed it out. She looked like an Australian primary school teacher. Eternal Light's mouth fell open in astonishment: engrossed in his pious book, he hadn't even noticed I was smoking. I thought it best to make a quick exit – things could quickly deteriorate with these two jokers. Where had Rudi disappeared to? I slowly wandered around the market before spotting him deep in conversation with one of the Azraelians.

On the way to Famara, he gave me some further information. According to Azrael, the Anakim had not only created mankind, they had also created all life on earth. 'I don't see why we should be grateful to them for that . . .' I sniggered under my breath. It was not de facto an absurd notion; I'd come across theories on the extraterrestrial origins of life on earth before, spores filled with Martian bacteria or something like that. I didn't know whether such theories had been proven or refuted, and to be honest, I didn't really give a shit. The road snaked upward in hairpin bends as

far as the Ermita de las Nieves before sloping down to
the coast. As we arrived at the summit, I realised that
the climate on the other side of the island was
noticeably different. Huge grey clouds covered the
sky, the wind whistled between the rocks.

Famara offers the visitor a depressing glimpse of a
failed beach resort. It is here that the Norwegian
influence is most keenly felt. A number of flaxen-
haired homeowners still stubbornly try to cultivate a
garden aesthetic (although the sky is constantly
overcast, it never rains in Famara any more than it
does elsewhere on the island); they leaned on their
rakes and watched as we passed. Everywhere there
were little signs which read 'Rooms to Rent'. Ours
was virtually the only car on the seafront; café owners,
attracted by the noise of the engine, came out and
stood in their doorways, full of hope. The beach itself
was, it must be said, magnificent: an immense sandy
cove several kilometres long; but the sea was too grey
and too choppy to be inviting to bathers and no one
could be expected to spend an entire month's holiday
windsurfing. Not a sound indicated any human
presence: not a telephone or a radio, nothing. Half
buried in the sand, pleasure boats rusted slowly.

None of this affected my good mood in the least; it

was at that point that I realised that I was growing to love this island. Rudi, on the other hand, seemed terribly disappointed, almost in tears. 'Oh, well . . .' I felt obliged to say, 'I suppose it's hardly surprising there aren't many people. When it's cloudy like this and the sea is too rough, people get bored.' By mutual agreement, we headed back towards the volcanoes.

The further south we drove, the more spectacular the landscapes became. Just past the Tinajo intersection, Rudi suggested that we stop. I joined him on the hard shoulder which overlooked a sheer drop. He stood there, his gaze fixed, as though hypnotised. We looked out over a barren desert. In front of us, a huge fissure, several metres wide, snaked as far as the horizon, cutting through the grey surface of the earth's crust. The silence was absolute. This, I thought, is what the world will look like when it dies.

Later, perhaps, there might be a resurrection. The wind and the sea would assail the rocks, breaking them down into dust and sand; little by little soil would form. Plants would appear – and, somewhat later, animals. Right now, however, there was nothing but rock – and a road carved out by man.

In the car, Rudi explained why the Azraelians were here on the island. Philippe Leboeuf had first thought to build the embassy which would welcome the aliens in Switzerland, or perhaps the Bahamas – in short, his thinking had been guided by economic factors. Then, a fortuitous holiday to Lanzarote had put him back on the right track. First contact had taken place in the scorched mountains of Sinai; the second in an extinct crater at Puy de Dôme. The third would take place here, in the midst of the volcanoes, in the land of the ancient peoples of Atlantis.

I considered this information for a while. It was true that if aliens were to appear one day, this would be an ideal backdrop to the CNN report; all the same, I was having a bit of trouble swallowing it.

The sun was setting as we reached Geria. A steep valley, it wends its way between hills of rocks and gravel which ranged in colour from dark purple to black. Over the centuries, the people of the island had built low semicircular walls with these stones; within the shelter of these low walls they had dug deep holes in the gravel. Into each hole, sheltered from the wind, they planted a vine. Volcanic rock makes an excellent soil and there is good sun; the grapes harvested here make a heady, fragrant muscat. The determination needed to undertake the work was impressive. Lanzarote was born out of an utter geological catastrophe; but here, in the few square kilometres of this valley, we were witnessing an abstract terrain, recreated to man's purposes.

I suggested to Rudi that we take a picture; but, no, the idea didn't seem to interest him. In fact, nothing seemed to interest him; he seemed to me to be in a bad way. None the less, he agreed to stop for a wine tasting.

'Tomorrow, we could ask the German girls to come with us . . .' I suggested, a glass of muscat in hand.

'Which German girls?'

'Pam and Barbara.'

He thought hard, his brows knitted; clearly, he couldn't really remember.

'Why not . . .' he said finally. 'But they're dykes, aren't they?' he asked after a moment.

'So what?' I said petulantly. 'Dykes are nice . . . well, sometimes they're nice.'

He shrugged his shoulders as though he couldn't care less. When we got back to the hotel, it was dark. Rudi went to bed straight away; he wasn't hungry, he told me. He apologised, he was sorry, maybe it was just that he was a bit tired, whatever . . . So I went into the restaurant to look for Pam and Barbara alone.

7

As I expected, they enthusiastically agreed; but they had ideas of their own about how the day would be spent. They wanted to go to the nudist beach at Papagayo. You have to take the Germans as you find them, I said to Rudi the following morning, but if you go along with their little idiosyncrasies, you're generally rewarded, for the most part they're decent girls. Still, I insisted we make a short detour to the beach at El Golfo where a huge jagged rock rises out of the sea, a whole lot of strange colours – anyway, it's very beautiful. In the event, everyone agreed and Rudi, who was much more cheerful now, took at least thirty photos. We had lunch in a bar at Playa Blanca: tapas and white wine. By now a little enthusiastic, Pam took us into her confidence. Yes, they were lesbian, but not *exclusively* lesbian. Heh heh! I thought. Then she wanted to know if we were queers. 'Eh . . . no,' I said. Rudi was having difficulty finishing his octopus.

He stabbed the last piece with a toothpick, looked up and answered absent-mindedly: 'No, no, me neither . . . Not as far as I'm aware.'

After our stop at Playa Blanca, we drove along the coast road for about ten minutes, then we turned left towards the Punta de Papagayo. Everything was fine for the first couple of kilometres, then the road suddenly deteriorated before turning into a dirt track. I stopped the car and suggested that Rudi take the wheel. We had a 4x4, but I've always hated four-wheel drives, off-road driving and that kind of thing. I've never been fascinated by anti-skid mechanisms or anti-lock brakes. Give me a motorway and a good Mercedes and I'm a happy man. The first thing that occurs to me when I have the misfortune to take the wheel of a four-wheel drive, is to heave the fucking thing into a ravine and continue on foot.

The track wound slowly, in wide meanders, up the steep hill. It was a difficult climb, we couldn't get the car above five kilometres an hour and clouds of ochre dust swirled around us. I glanced over my shoulder: Pam and Barbara didn't seem in the least bit bothered by the route, they bobbed gently on their plastic seats.

At the summit, there was a surprise waiting for us.

A small booth, like a customs post, with a sign above it reading 'PROTECTED AREA', blocked the path. 'Here we go,' I thought. To go any further, we had to pay an entrance fee of 1,000 pesetas, in exchange for which we received a little brochure warning that this was a world ecological reserve and listing a number of prohibitions. I read in disbelief that there was a fine of 20,000 pesetas and up to six months' imprisonment just for picking up a pebble. As for plants, don't even think about it; in any case, there weren't any plants. In fact, the landscape didn't seem particularly remarkable; actually, it was a lot less beautiful than what we had seen the previous day. We clubbed together to pay the entrance fee. 'They've got it sussed . . .' I whispered to Rudi. 'Pick any old spot in the middle of nowhere, let the road go to hell and stick up a "PROTECTED AREA" sign and people are bound to come. Then all you've got to do is set up a toll booth and you're in business.'

A few hundred metres further on, an intersection fanned out like a starburst, with five or six paths. Playa Colorada, Playa del Gato, Playa Graciosa, Playa Mujeres . . . there was no point trying to choose between them. 'Take the one in the middle,' I said to Rudi. A little further there was another junction, and then a third. Suddenly, we could see the sea. Here, at the southernmost tip of the island, it was a perfect blue. In the distance, through the heat haze, we could just make out the sandy shores of Fuertaventura. We rounded two sharp bends and the track came to a halt on a deserted cove. Black rocks framed a sandy slope which plunged steeply towards the sea.

I immediately went for a swim with Pam and Barbara. Though they were a few metres away, I didn't really feel excluded from their games. I thought it might be worth my while to stay in the water a little longer. I was right, when I came out to dry myself, they were already entwined on their towels. Pam had placed her hand on Barbara's pubis. Barbara parted her thighs a little. Rudi was sitting a few metres away looking sullen; he still had his shorts on. I spread my towel about a metre from Barbara's. She leaned towards me. '*You can come closer . . .*' she said in English. I moved closer. Pam crouched over Barbara's face, offering her pussy to be licked. She had a pretty little shaven pussy, with a well-shaped slit, not too long. I stroked Barbara's breasts lightly. Their roundness was so pleasant to the touch that I closed my eyes for a long moment. I opened them again, moved my hand to her stomach. Her pussy was very different, blonde and bushy with a fat clitoris. The sun was high. Pam was close to coming, she gave strange little cries, the sort you'd imagine a mouse might make. Blood rushed suddenly to her breasts and she came in a growl of ecstasy. Then she took a deep breath and sat back on the sand.

'Did you enjoy that?' she asked, though with a hint of irony.

'Very much. Honestly, very much.'

'I can see . . .' I still had a hard-on. She took my cock in her hand and began to jerk me off with a friendly to-and-fro action. 'I don't really do penetration any more, but Barbara does.'

'I'd love to . . .' I felt like a complete fool. 'But I haven't got any condoms.'

She burst out laughing and said something in German to Barbara. 'It doesn't matter . . .' she said, getting to her feet enthusiastically, 'I'm sure we'll think of some way of dealing with you. Let's go for a swim.'

As I got up, I noticed that Rudi had disappeared. His towel was still where he had left it. I hesitated for a moment, then thought: *Am I my brother's keeper?* In any case, he couldn't have gone far. *'Your friend looks sad . . .'* Barbara said to me in English when we were in

the water. *'Yes . . . his life is not funny.'* That was the
least you could say. She looked at me affectionately; I
racked my brains but couldn't think of anything else to
say. I've always had problems with English, after three
sentences I'm completely lost, but what can I do? In
any case, Barbara didn't seem any better with the
language. When I dried off, I laid my towel next to
hers and just went for it.

'You look a good girl. May I lick your pussy?'

'Ja, ja!' the words might not have been exactly
right but she'd clearly got the gist of it.

She got up and squatted over my face – it was
obviously a position she was familiar with. First, I
lightly caressed the outer labia with my tongue, then
I pushed two fingers inside her – to no great effect: she
was clearly very clitoral. I gave her little nub a quick
flick of my tongue; she breathed more heavily. She had
a wonderful musky taste, only slightly masked by the
taste of salt. Her large breasts hung above my face. I
had just begun to speed up the pace of my tongue-
flicks when I felt her stiffen; she straightened up
slightly. I turned my head: Rudi was standing a couple
of metres away, melancholy and pot-bellied.

'Come!' Barbara called cheerfully. *'Come with us!'*

He shook his head, I thought I heard him mumble

something like: 'No, no, it's not that . . .' then he sat down heavily on the sand. After a moment of embarrassment, Barbara parted her thighs again, bringing her sex to my mouth. I placed my hands on her buttocks and once again began to lick with mounting passion; after a while I closed my eyes to savour the taste. Shortly afterwards, I felt Pam's small mouth close over the head of my cock. The sun was still very hot; it was divine. Pam had a very particular way of sucking, almost without moving her lips, running her tongue around the glans, sometimes very quickly, sometimes exquisitely slowly.

Barbara's excitement continued to mount, her cries were becoming really loud. At the moment of orgasm, she arched her back violently and let out a long scream. I opened my eyes: her head back, her hair loose, her breasts pointing skyward, she had the imposing beauty of a goddess. I myself felt myself close to coming in Pam's mouth.

'Pam, stop . . .' I begged.

'Don't you want to come now?'

Barbara lay down on her back, her breathing laboured. 'OK, go on . . .' I said finally to Pam. She signalled for me to come closer to Barbara and put her hand on my cock again, then said something in

German to her friend. 'She says you lick pretty well, for a man . . .' she said before placing her other hand on my balls. I groaned softly. She pointed my cock towards Barbara's chest and began to jerk me off with short, staccato strokes, her fingers forming a ring at the base of the glans. Barbara looked at me and smiled; just as she pressed her hands against the sides of her breasts, accentuating their roundness, I ejaculated violently over her chest. I was in a sort of trance, my eyes blurred, I watched as through a mist as Pam spread my come over her partner's breasts. I lay back on the sand, exhausted; my vision seemed increasingly blurred. Pam began to lick the come off Barbara's breasts. It was an infinitely touching gesture; tears welled up in my eyes. I fell asleep right there, my arm around Barbara's waist, crying tears of joy.

Pam shook me awake. I opened my eyes again. The sun was setting over the sea. 'We should head back . . .' she said, 'We have to go back, Mr Frenchman.' I got dressed automatically, in a mood of happy relaxation. 'What a beautiful afternoon . . .' I said quietly as we walked back to the car. She nodded. 'We could buy some condoms,' I added, 'I saw a chemist's at Playa Blanca.' 'If it makes you happy . . .' she said gently.

Rudi and Barbara were waiting for us by the car. Pam sat in the front. In the twilight, the ochre of the plateau veered towards something warmer, almost orange. We drove in silence for several kilometres, then Pam said to Rudi: 'I hope we didn't shock you back there.'

'Not at all, Mademoiselle.' He smiled sadly. 'It's just that I'm a bit. A bit . . . You'll have to forgive me,' he finished abruptly.

As usual when we got back at the hotel, Rudi wanted to go straight to bed, but Pam insisted that the four of us have dinner together; she knew a restaurant to the north of the island.

The potatoes in Lanzarote are small and wrinkled and their flesh is very flavoursome. The cooking method – particular to the island – involves placing them at the bottom of small earthenware pots, into which a little highly salted water is poured. As the water evaporates, it coats the potatoes in a salt crust, sealing in all the flavour.

Pam and Barbara lived near Frankfurt. Barbara worked at a hairdresser's. I didn't quite understand what Pam did, but it was something in the financial sector, and much of the work could be done over the Internet.

'I don't think of myself as *lesbian*,' said Pam. 'Barbara and I are together, that's all.'

'Are you faithful?'

She blushed a little. 'Yes . . . now, yes, we're faithful to each other. Except from time to time with a man, but that's different, it doesn't mean anything.'

I glanced at Barbara, who was eating her potatoes with relish. Sitting opposite her, Rudi wasn't really eating at all, he was just picking at his food; he wasn't taking part in the conversation either, it was beginning to depress me, I couldn't think what to do with him. Barbara looked up at him and smiled. *'You should eat. It's very good,'* she said. Obediently, he speared a potato with his fork.

They were intending to settle in Spain, Pam told me, as soon as it became possible for her to do all her work over the Internet. Not in Lanzarote, probably in Majorca or on the Costa Brava.

'There are problems with Germans in Majorca,' I said.

'I know . . .' she said. 'It'll blow over. In any case, we're all part of Europe. The Germans don't want to stay in Germany any more, it's cold and horrible and they think there are too many Turks. As soon as they have a bit of money, they head south; there's no stopping them.'

'Turkey will probably be part of Europe soon,' I commented, 'then the Germans can settle there.'

She smiled broadly. 'They might well just do that . . . Germans are weird. I'm very fond of them, even if they are my compatriots. In Majorca, we have a lot of German friends and Spanish friends. You could come and visit if you'd like.'

Then she explained that she and Barbara wanted to have children. Barbara would probably be the one to give birth as she was keen to give up her job. They weren't thinking of using artificial means for the conception; it would be easier simply to ask a male friend, they knew a few men who would be happy to impregnate Barbara.

'That doesn't surprise me . . .' I said.

'Would you be interested?' she asked me, bluntly.

I was speechless; I felt terribly embarrassed. Because yes, though the thought had never crossed my mind until now, I *was* interested. She patted my hand gently. 'We'll talk about it later . . . We'll talk to Barbara about it.'

To defuse this momentary embarrassment, we talked about Spanish women; we agreed that they were worth fucking. Not only do they enjoy sex, but they often have large breasts and in general they're nice girls, uncomplicated and very modest, unlike Italian women – who are so preoccupied with how beautiful they are that they become unfuckable, in spite of their otherwise excellent qualifications. This safe conversation took us up to dessert – a cinnamon crème brûlée; then we ordered a bottle of Pernod. Despite my repeated glances in his direction, I hadn't managed to get Rudi involved in the conversation; he sat silent, almost stupefied, in his chair. In desperation, I said: 'What about the Belgians? What can we say about the Belgians?'

He looked at me almost in terror, as though I had opened up an abyss in front of him.

'Belgians are an extremely scatological, deeply perverse people, happy to wallow in their own humiliation,' he began rhetorically. 'As I said the first time we spoke: I believe Belgium is a country which should never have existed. I remember seeing a poster in a centre for alternative culture with the simple slogan: "Bomb Belgium"; I couldn't have agreed more. When I married a Moroccan, it was to escape the Belgians.

'Then she left me . . .' he went on, his voice

different now. 'She went back to her stupid fucking Islam, she took my daughters away and I'll never see them again.'

Barbara looked at him with such compassion that I saw a tear well in Rudi's eye. She didn't understand a word, all she understood was his tone of voice; but that was enough for her to realise that this was a man at the end of his tether.

What else was there to say? Nothing, obviously. I poured Rudi another Pernod.

On the way back, we didn't say much. In the lobby of the hotel, Pam and Barbara kissed Rudi several times on each cheek to wish him good night. I shook his hand, made a vague attempt to pat him on the shoulder. It has to be said, men aren't very good at this kind of thing.

I felt a bit of an idiot with my condoms as I headed towards the German girls' room; I was feeling a bit low. Pam explained the situation to Barbara, who interrupted her and launched into a long tirade in German. 'She says you're wrong, this is precisely the right time for us to make love, it will do all three of us good . . .' said Pam placing her hand on my cock. She unbuttoned my trousers and pushed them down to the floor. Barbara undressed completely, knelt in front of me and took me in her mouth. It was extraordinary: she closed her lips round the tip of my penis and slowly, centimetre by centimetre, took it into her throat; then she began to move her tongue. After two minutes, I felt that I couldn't hold back any longer. 'Now!' I said in a loud voice. Barbara understood immediately, fell back on the bed and parted her thighs. I slipped on a condom and entered her. Pam, who was sitting beside us, played with herself as she watched us. I pushed into Barbara deeply, slowly at first, then more quickly; Pam stroked Barbara's breasts. She was enjoying this and was clearly completely relaxed, but she was still a long way from orgasm when Pam made her move. Placing her hand on her friend's pussy, she began to rub Barbara's clitoris in short quick strokes with her index and middle fingers. I stopped moving. The walls of Barbara's cunt contracted around my prick in rhythm with her breathing. Mischievously, Pam took my balls in her other hand and began to squeeze them gently as she speeded up her movements. She did all this with such skill that Barbara and I came at exactly the same time, I with a short, passionate cry, she with a long, hoarse growl.

I put my arms around Pam and planted little kisses

on her neck and shoulders while Barbara began to lick her. She came a little later in a series of little high-pitched squeals. I was exhausted and headed over to the spare bed — a child's bed, actually — while Pam and Barbara continued to embrace and lick each other on the double bed. I was naked and happy. I knew I was going to get a good night's sleep.

8

The following day we had nothing planned and had made no arrangements to meet; even so, by eleven o'clock, I was beginning to worry that there was no sign of Rudi. I went and knocked on his door, but there was no answer. I asked at reception where a clerk told me that he had left early that morning and had taken all his things; he didn't know where he'd gone. Yes, he had definitely checked out.

I was in the process of relaying the news to Pam and Barbara who were sunning themselves by the pool, when the receptionist came up to me with an envelope. Rudi had left a message. I went up to my room to read it. The letter was several pages long, written in black ink in tiny, neat, precise handwriting.

Dear Sir,
In the first place, I would like to thank you for having treated me like a human being these

last few days. This may seem unremarkable to you; to me, it is not. You probably don't know what it's like to be a cop; you don't realise the extent to which we are a society apart, inward-looking, with our own rituals, regarded with contempt and suspicion by the populace at large. Doubtless you know even less about how it feels to be Belgian. You cannot imagine the violence – real or latent – the mistrust and the fear we are faced with in the most simple everyday encounters. For example, try asking for directions from a passer-by on the street in Brussels; the results will surprise you. In Belgium, we no longer constitute what is commonly called a society; we no longer have anything in common but humiliation and fear. I realise that this tendency is common to all European countries; but for a variety of reasons (which a historian would no doubt be well placed to explain), this process of deterioration is already alarmingly serious in Belgium.

Secondly, I would like to say again that your behaviour with your German friends did not shock me in the slightest. My wife and I, in the last two years of our marriage, regularly frequented what are generally referred to as clubs for 'non conformist' couples. She enjoyed this, as did I. Even so, as the months passed – I don't know why exactly – things began to go awry. What had, at the beginning, been a joyous party with no taboos, gradually turned into a joyless exercise in depravity, there was something very cold and very narcissistic about it. We were unable to get out in time. In the end, we even endured humiliating situations where we allowed ourselves to be passive spectators to displays by absolute sexual monsters, encounters in which we could no longer participate, given our age. It is perhaps this which pushed my wife – an intelligent, sensitive and deeply cultured woman – towards the monstrous and reactionary solutions of Islam. I do not know whether this catastrophe was inevitable; but when I think back on it – and I have thought of little else for five years – I cannot see how I could have prevented it.

Sexuality is a powerful force, so powerful that any relationship which does not embrace it is necessarily incomplete. There is a body

barrier just as there is a language barrier. Being
men, you and I, our relations were reduced to
a limited exchange, and I can absolutely understand your intentions in initiating an encounter
with Pam and Barbara; I understand it, and I
thank you for it. But for me, it is, sadly, a little
late. The worst thing about depression is that
it makes it impossible even to contemplate the
sexual act, even though it might be the only
thing which would assuage the terrible feeling
of anguish that comes with depression. You
cannot imagine how difficult it was simply for
me to decide to take this holiday.

I know that what follows will upset you,
and that you will feel in part responsible. But
that is not so, and I would like to repeat that
you did everything in your power to bring me
back to a 'normal' life. To put it briefly, I have
decided to join the Azraelian sect. I should
mention that I had already been in touch with
members of the sect in Belgium; but I didn't
know that Lanzarote was an important centre.
In a way, it was that which helped me decide to
take the plunge. I know that to Westerners,
joining a 'sect', and the renunciation of a

certain sort of individual freedom which that entails, is always thought of as a dramatic personal failing. I would like to try to explain to you why, in this case, I think the accusation unjustified.

What can we expect from life? This is a question which seems to me impossible to evade. Every religion, in its own way, attempts to answer this question, and the non-religious pose the question in almost precisely the same terms.

The answer given by the Azraelians is radically new in that it proposes that everyone, from this very moment, can enjoy physical immortality. What happens is this: a skin sample is taken from each new member; this sample is kept at a very low temperature. The sect is in constant contact with the biotechnology companies that are most advanced in the field of human cloning. According to leading specialists, the project will be achievable in a matter of years.

Let us take this a little further. Azrael offers the immortality of thoughts and memories – by transferring the contents of memory to an intermediary medium, which in due course will be transferred into the brain of the clone. This suggestion, it is true, sounds like science fiction inasmuch as, at the moment, we have no idea how such a thing might be implemented.

Be that as it may, it seems strange to refer to an organisation as a 'sect' when it offers such innovative and technologically radical answers to questions which conventional religions have dealt with more irrationally and metaphorically. The weak point of their doctrine is, obviously, that it depends on the existence of the *Anakim*, the extra-terrestrials which supposedly created life on earth hundreds of millions of years ago. But, aside from the fact that this is by no means an absurd hypothesis, it should be noted that, for one reason or another, human societies have always had great difficulty in organising themselves without reference to a higher principle.

From a financial perspective, the accusation that the Azraelians are a 'sect' doesn't hold either. Each new member gives

20 per cent of his income to the community – no more, no less. Naturally, if he decides to leave his home in order to join a collective, the contribution can be greater than that. For my part, this is what I have decided to do. My house is no longer of any interest to me, I have not felt at home there since my wife and my daughters left. In any case, the area has become a dangerous one, where every day I am humiliated because of my position as a police officer. So I am going to sell it and join the Azraelian community in Belgium.

All this may seem very sudden, and I will not pretend that it is a decision based on mature reflection, taken after a considerable period spent weighing up the pros and cons. But what I would like you to understand is that, with my life the way it is, I don't really have anything to lose.

As I close this long letter, it remains for me to thank you for your patience and your humanity, and to wish all the best in life to you and your family.

Yours affectionately,
Rudi.

9

I put down the letter, devastated. So they were going to get their hands on the money from the sale of his house. A lifetime of saving and borrowing, and now this. On the other hand, perhaps they were sincere. That's the problem with sects, until the scandal breaks, you can never be sure of anything.

I summarised the contents of the letter for Pam and Barbara. By mutual consent, we decided not to take a trip that day. I went back to the hire company to return the car, then spent the rest of the day by the pool with them. Pam had finished the Marie Desplechin, which she hadn't really liked. I suggested she read a book by Emmanuel Carrère, *L'Adversaire*; obviously, I only had the French edition with me, but if she came across something difficult, I could always explain it to her. For myself, I couldn't bring myself to read; I lay on a sunlounger and watched the clouds as they flitted across the sky. My head felt pretty much empty, and it seemed to me better that way.

That night, the three of us slept, arms wrapped around each other, on the double bed, though nothing sexual happened. As though we simply needed to protect ourselves; as though we could feel some dark presence, some evil subterranean force moving about the island. On the other hand, perhaps Azrael was a good prophet, perhaps his ideas would lead to the betterment of the human condition. One thing was certain, in any event: what had happened to Rudi could have happened to any one of us; no one was safe any more. No social status, no relationship could any longer be considered certain. We were living in a time in which any Advent, any Armageddon was possible.

The following morning, Pam and Barbara came with me to the airport. None of us had mentioned the subject of Barbara having a baby; but as we were saying our goodbyes by the walk-through metal detector, I felt, as she hugged me to her, a singular emotion. Pam waved to me, I walked down the corridor towards the departure lounge.

As the plane took off, I took one last look at this landscape dotted with volcanoes which glowed deep red in the dawn light. Were they comforting, or, conversely, threatening? I couldn't say. But whatever they were, they represented the possibility of regeneration, of a new beginning. A regeneration by fire. The plane was climbing now. Then it turned on a wing towards the ocean.

It was cold in Paris, everything was as disagreeable as ever. What was the point? We know what life is like, the ins and outs of it. I would just have to readapt to the endless winter; and to the twentieth century which, seemed similarly reluctant to end. Deep down, I understood the choice Rudi had made. That said, he was wrong about one thing: it's perfectly possible to live without expecting anything of life; in fact, it's the most common way. In general, people stay at home, they're happy that their phone never rings; and when it does, they let the answering machine pick up. No news is good news. In general, that's what people are like; I am too.

Even when there is nothing left to expect from life, there is still something to fear. I'd noticed that there were more and more dealers in my area. I decided to move again, closer to the Assemblée Nationale; I told people it was so that I could be closer to work, but actually it was so that I could live in a heavily policed area. I really couldn't see the point of getting myself stabbed by some fucker in need of a fix.

The months passed. Pam and Barbara wrote me a number of postcards and I wrote back; but we didn't quite get round to meeting up again. From time to time, I would happen on an article about the Azraelians and cut it out. Actually, such articles were pretty rare; it's a very inconspicuous sect. The longest article, which appeared in *Le Nouvel Observateur* on 23 March, included a photo of a dozen men wearing white robes and embroidered stoles. In the middle stood Philippe Leboeuf, alias Azrael. With touching pride, they were gathered round a small polystyrene model of the future 'city to welcome extra-terrestrials'. Rudi wasn't in the photo. The project was going ahead, according to the article; they had come to some agreement with the local authorities to build it in Lanzarote; construction was set to begin in the coming months.

On 18 June, 2000, a conference aimed at promoting the cause of human cloning was held in Montreal. On the platform, united for the first time, the prophet Azrael and the American geneticist Richard Seed

announced the creation of a joint facility, free of all
religious ties – Dr Seed still claimed to be a Christian
and a Methodist. It subsequently transpired that a
group of investors from the Valiant Venture Limited
Corporation had already amassed several million
dollars for the construction of the laboratory. The
writer, Maurice G. Dantec, who was present,
described the event to a local paper in glowing terms;
this was the first serious intellectual backing for the
cause. Immediately, a heated debate began in
'Rebonds', the letters page of *Libération*, until the
school holidays put an end to it.

The scandal broke in December, a few days before Christmas. A new paedophile ring had been uncovered in Belgium; this time, members of the Azraelian sect were implicated. Paedophiles, sects and the coming holiday season were all combined in a fanatical media feeding frenzy. *France-Soir* broke new ground with a front page – no photos – consisting of a litany of names from Aïcha (eleven years old) to William (nine). Superimposed in yellow, across the whole page, was the headline 'GROOMED FOR SEX'. *Détective*, anxious to condense the salient facts of the affair into a single sentence, ran the rather bizarre headline: 'CHILD ORGIES AMONG ALIEN HUNTERS'. The case was heard at the Palais de Justice in Brussels: radio and TV stations, familiar with the location from the Dutroux case, dispatched experienced crews to cover the case on location.

It soon became apparent that all the Azraelians,

whether married or not, had had very free sexual relations, and that orgies which could include up to a hundred people regularly took place at the organisation's Brussels headquarters. The children of the disciples were not excluded from such scenes; at times they were merely spectators, at others participants. No evidence of violence nor of coercion of the children was found; but it was clearly a case of the corruption of minors. The witness statements were unambiguous: 'When Daddy's friends came to stay at the house I would go upstairs and give them blow jobs,' reported twelve-year-old Aurélie. Nicole, forty-seven, could clearly remember having incestuous sex with her two sons, now twenty-one and twenty-three, for years.

What struck commentators most was the attitude of the defendants. The paedophile is typically a guilty creature, prostrate and completely defeated. Repulsed by his own actions, he is terrorised by the uncontrollable nature of his impulses. Either he hides behind fierce denials, or he can't wait to be punished, he wallows in his guilt and his remorse, demands treatment, gratefully agrees to chemical castration. Nothing of the sort was to be found among the Azraelians. Not only did they feel no remorse, they considered themselves to be part of some sort of evolving moral avant-garde and declared that society would be much better off if everyone had the integrity to behave as they did. 'We have given pleasure to our children. From earliest childhood we have taught them to experience pleasure and to give pleasure to others. We have completely fulfilled our duty as parents.' This, more or less, was their collective position.

Rudi was among the defendants. His case was not the most serious, but it was the one which had sparked the scandal. He was accused of molesting an eleven-year-old Moroccan girl named Aïcha. 'He used to take my clothes off and kiss me all over and he'd go down on me,' Aïcha told the investigating officers. It was her mother, a former member of the sect, who had lodged the complaint. Well, well, I thought. Rudi never did have much luck with Moroccans. The Muslim community was baying for his blood, especially as he was a former police officer (naturally he had been thrown out of the force as soon as the scandal broke); he had to be assigned a bodyguard. 'She used to say I was nice, sometimes she was the one who asked me to go down on her . . .' he declared to the investigating officers, sobbing all the while.

On 30 December, Philippe Leboeuf, who was not

among the accused, went to Brussels where he held a long-awaited press conference. The journalists who turned up were not disappointed: it was pretty explosive. Azrael gave his wholehearted support – and then some – to the actions of his Belgian disciples. Sex in all its forms was permitted, even encouraged, between members of the sect, regardless of age, gender or family relationships. All of this was pleasing and excellent in the sight of the Anakim. 'He doesn't know what he's letting himself in for – they'll ban them completely,' muttered the correspondent from *Le Figaro.* The prophet seemed to be in fine form, his slightly greying beard glowed in the spotlights. Sensing the general bewilderment, he seized the moment to step up the argument, denouncing Jesus Christ and Mohammed as impostors and on the other hand claiming Moses as a disciple.

'Nevertheless, what you're suggesting to your disciples is a far cry from the Ten Commandments,' commented the editor of *Le Soir,* interrupting for the first time.

Azrael jumped at the chance to expound his point of view. Moses, he explained, truly had been visited by the extraterrestrials, the Anakim; but he had misunderstood their message; hence the absurdity that was the Decalogue. The centuries which had followed were time wasted. Happily, he, the first true successor, had come to correct Moses' prophecies.

'This is ridiculous, he's just winding us up – it's a publicity stunt,' muttered the correspondent from *Paris-Match*.

Indeed, in the hours following the broadcast, visits to their Internet site soared and requests for information about the sect poured in. Leboeuf was on to a winner – particularly as he, personally, was irreproachable. In fact, for a guru, he had a particularly sedate, conservative family life. In the days that followed, the government, by contrast, appeared incompetent as they tried to field questions demanding whether the sect would be banned. These were criminal charges brought against private individuals; that they were members of a particular religious faith was a fact, but could not, under any circumstances, be the basis for a case against them.

Preparations for the case resumed. In fact, they progressed quite quickly, since no one contested the incriminating evidence, and the trial began shortly afterwards. Rudi sat in the dock in the Palais de Justice in Brussels flanked by some fifteen other disciples. Each was facing a lengthy prison sentence, but that didn't seem to affect them unduly. Rudi himself seemed serene, almost happy. In the photos, I noticed that he had started wearing big, square glasses with black frames; it was hardly a judicious choice. With his pot belly, his moustache and his big glasses, he was the one who brought to mind the classic image of the paedophile deviant. Public opinion was bitterly against the defendants and there were demonstrations almost every day in front of the Palais de Justice. There were calls for the reintroduction of the death penalty. One journalist tracked down Aïcha's father, who had been separated from her mother for several years. He stated that he wanted to see them 'cut the balls off' the man who had profaned his daughter's honour; he was quite willing to do the job himself.

Philippe Leboeuf appeared at the trial only as a witness. It seemed odd that he appeared at all, since he did not personally know any of the defendants. He had prepared a three-hour speech but the judge interrupted him after ten minutes. He had had the time, however, to announce that the Azraelian Church intended to lay the foundations for a new, sacred eroticism of the kind that had disappeared from the Western world thousands of years earlier. He also announced that, within Azraelian communities, schools for mutual masturbation were to be set up aimed at new members and small children. Masturbation, according to him, should be considered as the foundation stone of a new 'sensual catechism'. When he had finished giving evidence, Leboeuf walked over to the dock to shake hands with each of the defendants, but he was prevented from doing so by the police.

Undoubtedly because he looked like a typical paedophile, Rudi was often questioned by the press during the adjournments. He seemed to have become accustomed to it; he answered politely, benignly. Was he aware of the sentence he was facing? Yes, completely aware; but he did not regret anything. He had confidence in his country's justice system. He felt no remorse. 'I've never done anything but good to those around me . . .' he would say.

The trial dragged on, mostly because of the number of plaintiffs. That year, I signed up for a Nouvelles Frontières tour of Indonesia. I left Paris for Denpasar on 27 January. I wasn't there when the verdict was returned.

APPENDIX

The parish priest of Yaiza, Father Andrés Lorenzo Curbelo, recorded the events of the first few months of those six disastrous years. His account covers the period from 1 September 1730, to 28 December 1731.

'On the first day of September 1730, between nine and ten o'clock at night, the earth suddenly opened near Timanfaya, two miles from Yaiza. An enormous mountain emerged from the ground with flames coming from its summit. It continued burning for nineteen days. Some days later, a new abyss developed and an avalanche of lava rushed down over Timanfaya, Rodeo and part of Mancha Blanca. The lava extended over to the northern areas to begin with, running as fast as water, though it soon slowed down and ran like honey. On

7 September, a great rock burst upwards with a thunderous sound and the pressure of the explosion forced the lava going northwards to change direction, flowing then to the north-west and west-north-west. The lava torrent arrived, instantly destroying Maretas and Santa Catalina in the valley. On 11 September, the eruption became stronger. From Santa Catalina lava flowed to Mazo, covering the whole area and heading for the sea. It ran in cataracts for six continuous days, making a terrible noise. Huge numbers of dead fish floated about on the sea or were thrown on the shore. Then everything quietened, and the eruption appeared to have come to an end.

But on 18 October, three new fissures formed above Santa Catalina. Enormous clouds of smoke escaped, flowing over the whole island, accompanied by volcanic ashes, sand and debris. The clouds condensed and dropped boiling rain on the land. The volcanic activity remained the same for ten whole days with cattle dropping dead, asphyxiated by the vapours. By 30 October, everything had gone strangely quiet. Two days later, however, smoke and ashes reappeared and continued until the 10th of the month. Another flow of lava spewed out causing little damage as the surroundings were already scorched and devastated. A further avalanche started on the 27th, rushing at unbelievable speed towards the sea. It arrived at the shore on 1 December and formed a small island in the water where dead fish were found. On 16 December, the lava, which until then had been rushing towards the sea, changed direction, heading south-west, reaching Chupadero which, by the following day, had turned into a vast fire. This quickly devastated the fertile Vega de Uga, but went no further. New eruptions started on 7 January 1731, with spontaneous fireworks embellishing the sadness and desolation of the south. Powerful eruptions with incandescent lava and blue and red lighting crossed the night sky.

On 21 January, a gigantic mountain rose and sunk back into its crater on the same day with a terrifying sound, covering the island with stones and ashes. The fiery lava streams descended like rivers towards the sea with the ash, rocks and dense smoke making life impossible. That lava flow ceased on 27 January. But on the third day of February, a new cone threw out more lava towards the sea, which continued for twenty-five consecutive days. On 20 March new cones arose, with more eruptions continuing for eleven days. On 6 April, the same cones erupted again with even more fury. And on the 13th, two more mountains collapsed into their own craters making a frightful sound. By 1 May, the fire seemed to have burned out, only to start up again the following day, with yet another new cone rising and a current of lava threatening Yaiza itself. By 6 May, everything was quiet again and remained so for the rest of the month. However, on 4 June an enormous land rift took place which opened up three new craters and was accompanied by violent tremors and flames which terrified the local people. The eruption once more took place near Timanfaya. Different openings soon joined into one and the river of lava flowed down to the sea. A new cone appeared among the ruins of Maretas, Santa Catalina and

Timanfaya. A crater opened on the side of a mountain near Maso spewing out white fumes which had never been seen before. Towards the end of June 1731, all the western beaches and shores were covered with an incredible number of dead fish of all species – some with shapes which islanders had never known before. In the north-west, visible from Yaiza, a great mass of flames and smoke belched forth, accompanied by violent detonations. In October and November, more eruptions took place which worsened the islanders fears.

On Christmas Day 1731, the whole island shook with tremors, more violent than ever before.'